Little Mouse,
I Love You

pictures by caroline anstey
story by dugald steer

templar publishing

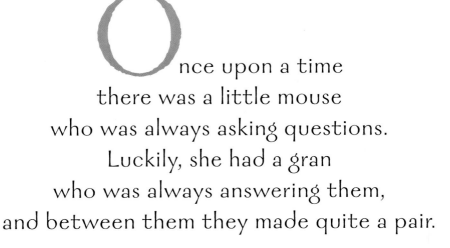

O nce upon a time
there was a little mouse
who was always asking questions.
Luckily, she had a gran
who was always answering them,
and between them they made quite a pair.

"Gran," asked Little Mouse one day,
"what is love?"
"Love?" laughed Gran.
"Oh, that's easy, Little Mouse!
Come for a walk and you'll soon see!"

Gran and Little Mouse set off
through the garden where Grandpa
was digging his vegetable patch.
"Shh," hushed Grandpa,
and pointed to where a mother wren
was teaching her chicks how to fly.

"Just like the way you and Gran
show me how to do things!"
whispered Little Mouse.

Beyond the garden gate lay
the wood, and it wasn't long before
Little Mouse spotted a mother squirrel
digging up some of the acorns
she had hidden in the autumn,
and sharing them among her children.

"Just like the way you share
the food you've cooked with me!"
exclaimed Little Mouse.

Passing through the wood
they reached the meadow.
Little Mouse liked it there because she
could watch all the rabbits scampering
about outside their burrows.
But today, one little rabbit
had cut his paw on a sharp stone
and a mother rabbit was lying beside
him to keep him company
while he got better.

"Just like the way
you sit by my bed with me
if I'm feeling poorly,"
cried Little Mouse.

There was a field near the
meadow, and Little Mouse
caught sight of a lamb who
was running up and down, looking
very frightened of a sheepdog.
But just then, a mother sheep strode
out of the flock and went over to the lamb,
who looked much happier as he nuzzled up to her.
"You see," smiled Gran, "that mother sheep was
just telling the lamb not to worry about the
sheepdog. He is there to look after them."

"Just like the way you
tell me not to worry
when I feel frightened,"
said Little Mouse.

When they had passed by the field,
Gran and Little Mouse came to the
duck pond, where there was a lot of quacking
and splashing as a brood of baby ducklings
scrambled after their mother.
"Those ducklings will grow up one day,
won't they?" said Little Mouse.

"Do you think their mummy will forget them
when she has new ones to look after?"
"No," said Gran. "She will
never forget a single one!"

"Just like the way you will
never forget me!" said Little Mouse.

By now it was beginning to get dark and,
as Gran and Little Mouse turned to go home,
they passed a barn. They could hear hooting
coming from inside, so Little Mouse peeped
around the door to see a mother owl
giving her little ones a tender peck before
she set out for the night.

"Just like the way you give me a
bedtime kiss," whispered Little Mouse.
"Yes," agreed Gran. "Although for the owls
it's a good morning one!"
And they both laughed.

Now that the evening had come,
Gran and Little Mouse walked home quickly and
they soon saw Grandpa, waving at the gate.

"Gran," said Little Mouse.
"All of those things I saw today – sort of
added together – do they make up love?"
"You know," said Gran, "I really think they do."